MARY ENGELBREIT'S
STORYBOOK FAVORITES
NURSERY AND FAIRY TALES

MARY ENGELBREIT'S
STORYBOOK FAVORITES
NURSERY AND FAIRY TALES

HARPER

An Imprint of HarperCollinsPublishers

TABLE of

CONTENTS

GOLDILOCKS and the THREE BEARS

ONCE UPON A TIME there were three bears: a great big Papa Bear, a medium-size Mama Bear, and a tiny, wee Baby Bear. One morning the three bears left their porridge to cool and went out walking.

While they were out, a little girl called Goldilocks
came upon the empty house. "I wonder who lives here,"
she said. She walked around to the back door and,
forgetting her manners, let herself into the kitchen.

On the table Goldilocks saw three bowls of porridge.

First she tasted the porridge in the great big bowl. But it was too hot.

Then she tried the porridge in the medium-size bowl. But it was too cold.

Then she tasted the porridge in the tiny, wee bowl. "This is just right!" said Goldilocks. And she ate it all up.

Then Goldilocks saw three chairs. First she sat in the great big chair. But it was too hard. Then she tried the medium-size chair. But it was too soft. Then she sat in the tiny, wee chair. "This is just right!" said Goldilocks. But no sooner did she say those words, than—*craaaack!* The tiny, wee chair broke into bits!

All this excitement made
Goldilocks sleepy, so she
climbed the stairs to the
bedroom. There she saw
three beds.

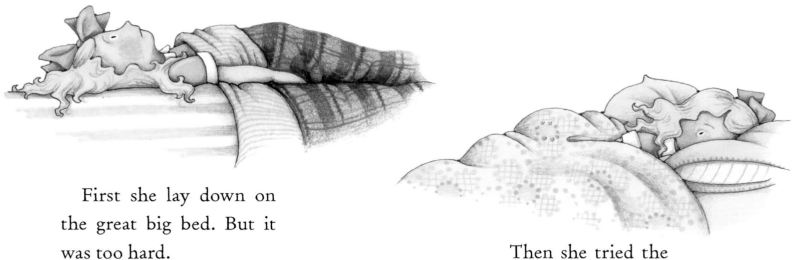

First she lay down on the great big bed. But it was too hard.

Then she tried the medium-size bed. But it was too soft.

Then she lay down on the tiny, wee bed. "This is just right!" said Goldilocks, and she soon fell fast asleep.

After a while, the three bears came back. When Papa Bear saw his bowl, he roared, "SOMEBODY'S BEEN EATING MY PORRIDGE!" And Mama Bear growled, "Somebody's been eating *my* porridge!" And Baby Bear squeaked, "Somebody's been eating *my* porridge and ate it all up!"

When Papa Bear saw his chair, he roared, "SOMEBODY'S BEEN SITTING IN MY CHAIR!"

And Mama Bear growled, "Somebody's been sitting in *my* chair!"

And Baby Bear—well, you know what happened to *his* chair. He squeaked, "Somebody's been sitting in *my* chair and broke it all to bits!"

So they all went into the bedroom, and when Papa Bear saw his bed he roared, "SOMEBODY'S BEEN SLEEPING IN MY BED!" And Mama Bear growled, "Somebody's been sleeping in *my* bed!" And Baby Bear squeaked, "Somebody's been sleeping in *my* bed—and there she is!"

Goldilocks heard the noise and woke with a start. When she saw the three bears, she sprang from the bed, jumped out the window, and ran home as fast as her legs would carry her.

Her mother and father were happy to see her. And the three bears lived happily ever after, too.

–2–
the THREE LITTLE PIGS

THERE ONCE were three little pigs who lived with their mother in a tiny house. As the little pigs grew bigger, the house grew smaller, and soon it came time for them to go out into the world and build houses of their own.

The first little pig hastily built her house of straw. The second little pig took a bit more time. He built a house of sticks. And the third little pig, who was smarter than the others, took the longest. She built a house of bricks.

Now, the first little pig was just sitting down to
breakfast in her new straw house when she heard the
voice of the Big Bad Wolf outside.

"Little pig, little pig, may I come in?" called the
Big Bad Wolf.

"Not by the hair on my chinny-chin-chin!" cried
the first little pig.

"Then I'll huff and I'll puff and I'll blow your house down," growled the Big Bad Wolf. And that's just what he did.

"Oh, help! Help!" squealed the first little pig, and do you know what? She ran to the house of sticks, where her brother took her in.

A little while later the brother and sister were just sitting down to lunch in the new stick house when they heard the Big Bad Wolf outside.

"Little pig, little pig, may I come in?" called the Big Bad Wolf.

"Not by the hair on my chinny-chin-chin!" cried the second little pig.

"Then I'll huff and I'll puff and I'll blow your house down," growled the Big Bad Wolf. And that's just what he did.

"Oh, help!" squealed the little pigs. And they ran and ran to the brick house, where their sister took them in.

A little while later the three little pigs were just

YOUR HOUSE DOWN!

sitting down to a bubbling-hot stew. Sure enough, they heard the Big Bad Wolf outside.

"Little pig, little pig, may I come in?" called the Big Bad Wolf.

"No, you may not," said the third little pig. "Not by the hair on my chinny-chin-chin."

"Then I'll huff and I'll puff and I'll blow your house down," growled the Big Bad Wolf.

"Go ahead and try," said the third little pig calmly.

The wolf huffed and he puffed, but try as he might, he could not blow that little brick house down.

Then the three little pigs heard noises on the roof, for the wolf had thought to try the chimney. Down tumbled the wolf, right into the cooking pot. He hopped out and scurried away, and that was the end of the Big Bad Wolf.

The three little pigs sang and played their favorite songs long into the night.

3

LITTLE RED RIDING HOOD

THERE ONCE was a little girl who always wore a red cloak with a hood, so everyone called her Little Red Riding Hood. One day her mother gave her a basket of biscuits to take to her granny, who was not feeling well.

Little Red Riding Hood set off, and she had not
gone very far before she met a wolf.

"Good morning," said the Wolf. "Where are you
going in such a beautiful red cloak?"

"I'm taking this basket of biscuits to my granny,
who is ill in bed," Little Red Riding Hood replied.

She knew she shouldn't
talk to strangers, but this
one seemed perfectly friendly.

"I hope your granny doesn't
live too far away," said the Wolf.

"Oh no," said Little Red Riding Hood. "She lives
in the cottage at the end of the path."

Now, the Wolf figured a weak old granny
would make an easy meal. So away he ran, taking
a shortcut straight to Granny's cottage. He
knocked at her door.

"Who's there?" Granny called.

"It's your little granddaughter,"
said the Wolf in a high voice.

"Lift the latch and let yourself in, dear," said Granny.

The Wolf lifted the latch, found Granny inside, and swallowed her in one gulp. Then he put on Granny's nightcap and climbed into her bed. Before long, Little Red Riding Hood knocked at the door.

"Lift the latch and let yourself in," called the Wolf.

Little Red Riding Hood lifted the latch and walked into the cottage. She took a few steps toward the bed and said, "Why, Granny, what big eyes you have."

"All the better to see you with, my dear," said the Wolf.

"And Granny, what big ears you have."
"All the better to hear you with, my dear."
"And Granny, what big teeth you have."

ALL THE BETTER
TO EAT YOU WITH,
MY DEAR!

"All the better to eat you with,
my dear!" growled the Wolf.
He jumped out of bed and ate Little Red
Riding Hood in one big gulp.

That might have been the end of Little Red Riding Hood, but luckily a woodcutter chopping wood near the cottage heard the Wolf's growls and came to look. When he saw the Wolf in Granny's glasses, he gave him a big scolding, and the Wolf let Little Red Riding Hood and her granny step out unharmed. Embarrassed, the Wolf ran away.

Do you remember the biscuits? They were still in the basket waiting—and they made a fine treat.

the EMPEROR'S NEW CLOTHES

Once there was an Emperor who wanted the best of everything—the tallest castle, the biggest army, the funniest jester, and especially the finest clothes. Knowing this, a clever tailor decided to play a trick on him.

The tailor came to the palace with his prettiest silks and satins. "Don't you have something better?" asked the Emperor. "Something nobody else has?"

"In this bag," the tailor said, "I have the finest cloth in the world. It is as thin as moonbeams and as light as air."

"Show me!" the Emperor demanded.

The tailor pretended to pull the cloth out of his bag. "Look at the colors!" he said. "Look at the pattern! Isn't it the loveliest thing you've ever seen?

"Anyone who wears it will feel as if he is wearing nothing at all. And there is one more thing." The tailor whispered in the Emperor's ear, "Only the wise can see this cloth. It is invisible to fools."

The Emperor could see nothing. But if I tell the tailor that, he thought, he'll think I am a fool! He'll know I'm not wise enough to be the Emperor! So the Emperor said, "Make me a suit of this cloth at once!"

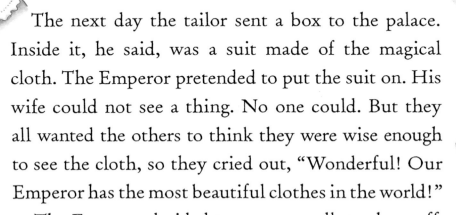

The next day the tailor sent a box to the palace. Inside it, he said, was a suit made of the magical cloth. The Emperor pretended to put the suit on. His wife could not see a thing. No one could. But they all wanted the others to think they were wise enough to see the cloth, so they cried out, "Wonderful! Our Emperor has the most beautiful clothes in the world!"

The Emperor decided to go on a walk to show off. Now, all the townspeople had heard of the Emperor's new clothes. They did not want to look like fools, so they clapped and cheered as if they could see what the Emperor was wearing.

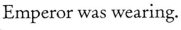

One little girl came onto her balcony. She could
see that the Emperor had nothing on. And she didn't
care if people thought she was foolish, so she said
loudly, "But he doesn't have any clothes on. The
Emperor has no clothes!"

People in the crowd heard. And they all realized
that *nobody* could see the Emperor's new clothes!

"The Emperor has no clothes!" they shouted.

The Emperor's soldiers heard. His servants heard. His wife heard.

"The Emperor has no clothes!" they gasped.

And the Emperor heard. Then he knew how the tailor had tricked him. He rushed home. For many weeks he hardly dared to show his face. And to this day people tell the story of a foolish Emperor who took a walk one day wearing no clothes at all!

5

HANSEL and GRETEL

There once lived a brother and sister called Hansel and Gretel. Their family was poor, and they only had stale bread to eat. One day Mother sent them out into the woods to pick wild strawberries for supper.

"The woods get dark quickly," Mother said. "Be sure you don't get lost."

Now Hansel was a clever boy, and Gretel was a clever girl. As they walked farther and farther into the woods, they dropped a trail of bread crumbs to follow back to their cottage.

Working together, Hansel and Gretel filled their basket with ripe red berries. By late afternoon they were ready to go home.

"Mother will be happy," Hansel said.

"But where are the bread crumbs?" Gretel cried.

The birds had eaten every crumb. There was no trail to lead the children home.

Lost and afraid, poor Hansel and Gretel at last ate the
berries. Trying to stay cheerful, the children made plans
for the morning, then fell asleep on the forest floor.

When the sun woke them, Hansel and Gretel set off through the woods. They'd wandered all day long when they came to a clearing, and there they saw a wonderful thing. It was a little cottage made of cake and candy! Hansel and Gretel were so hungry that they started breaking off bits of the house to eat.

They heard a strange voice whisper: "Nibble, nibble, like a mouse. Who is nibbling at my house?"

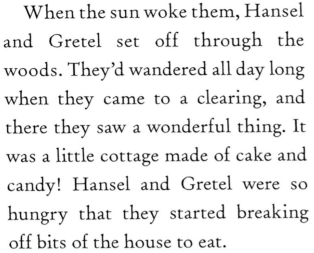

NIBBLE, NIBBLE, Like a Mouse, who is nibbling at my House?

Suddenly the door opened, and out came a very ugly woman who was really a witch. Hansel and Gretel were frightened, but the Witch spoke so sweetly and they were so hungry that they went with her into the house. Inside, the Witch fed them a delicious dinner, with all the foods and sweets they had ever dreamed of.

They were so full that they soon fell asleep. In the morning before they woke, the Witch lit a fire in the oven. "The boy first," she cackled. "He will be tasty!" For it was true—the Witch lured children to her cottage and then gobbled them up!

After the fire was lit, the Witch grabbed the sleeping Hansel and locked him in a cage behind the house. After that she came back and put Gretel to work.

"Get up and set the table!" she screeched. "I'm going to have a feast!"

Now clever Gretel saw Hansel in the cage, and as she set the table, she tried to think what to do.

"See if the oven is hot!" the Witch called to Gretel.

By now Gretel had a plan. So she said, "It is stone cold."

"That can't be," said the Witch, poking her head into the oven.

Quickly Gretel gave her a shove and banged the door shut. Then she set her brother free.

Hansel and Gretel ran away into the forest. Before long they heard their mother calling, searching for them. She was so happy to see her children that she wept with joy.

Then they all walked home together and sat down to eat. Their simple supper tasted so good!

the CITY MOUSE and the COUNTRY MOUSE

ONCE UPON A TIME there was a poor country mouse. Her cousin, the rich city mouse, came to visit.

"Wow!" said the City Mouse, seeing how her cousin lived. "You are really poor!"

"I don't have much to offer," said the Country Mouse. "But I'll go dig up something good to eat."

"Roots!" the City Mouse said when the Country Mouse returned. "At my house we don't have to *dig* for our dinner! Just this morning the Cook baked a cake!"

Now the Country Mouse felt very sorry for herself. "I'd like some cake!" she said.

So the two mice walked back to the city and into the fanciest house the Country Mouse had ever seen.

"This is the life!" said the City Mouse proudly. "And there's the cake!"

"It sure looks tasty," said the Country Mouse.

"We can eat our fill!" said the City Mouse. "As long as the Cook isn't looking," she added.

Just then—*Wham!*—the kitchen door opened and in came the Cook.

"Scat!" she cried, and the two cousins scurried into a hole.

"No problem," whispered the City Mouse. "We'll have another chance in just a second." But when they crept out again, the Cook chased them with a broom.

"Don't worry," said the City Mouse, all out of breath now. "That cake isn't going anywhere."

–7–

JACK and the BEANSTALK

THERE ONCE WAS a noble woman who had fallen on hard times. Her castle had been stolen away by a greedy giant, and now she lived in a cottage with her only son, Jack. He was a lazy boy—always dreaming, never working.

Mother and son grew poorer and poorer until they had nothing but a cow.

Jack's mother told him to sell the cow for a good price, and he agreed. But do you know what?

On the way into town, Jack met a strange little man, who gave him three magic beans in exchange for the cow. Jack thought his mother would be happy to have the beans—after all, they were magic!

"Three beans!" Jack's mother shouted when he got home. "You foolish boy!" Disgusted, she threw the beans out the window.

Now Jack felt sad, and he went straight to bed. But in the morning when he went to the window, he saw that the magic beans had sprung up into a huge vine! There was nothing to do but to climb it.

Higher and higher he climbed, until at last he reached the top of the vine and found himself looking at a castle that was high among the clouds.

Jack didn't know it, but this was the very castle that had been stolen from his mother when he was just a baby.

When Jack got there, he knocked. A giant woman
answered the door. After taking one look at him, she
said, "Please, please, run away! My husband is a cruel
giant!" But Jack was exhausted and hungry, so he
offered to work for food, and she let him in.

FEE FI FI FO FUM!

As he was finishing up his dinner, there came a deafening roar. Jack hid in a cupboard just as the Giant thundered in, bellowing, "Fee—Fi—Fo—Fum, I smell the blood of an Englishman!"

But the Giant's wife said, "It's the stew you smell."

"Hmph!" the Giant grunted, and he sat down to his giant supper. At last he finished eating, and his wife brought out a golden goose.

"Lay!" shouted the Giant. And the goose laid an egg of solid gold! The Giant amused himself for hours, commanding the goose to lay her golden eggs.

Finally the Giant's wife brought out a harp. The Giant said, "Play me a drink!" and a drink appeared. "Play me a pillow!" and a pillow appeared in the Giant's chair. "Play music!" and the harp played lovely music until, at last, the Giant fell asleep.

When the Giant was snoring loudly, Jack crept out of his hiding place, grabbed the golden goose and the harp, and started to run! But the harp twisted in Jack's grasp and started chiming, "Master! Master!"

Jack held tight to the goose and the harp and ran to the beanstalk as fast as he could go.

But the harp's cries woke the Giant. His feet shook the ground as he chased them! The beanstalk trembled with the terrible weight of him! As soon as Jack was safely on the ground, he cut the beanstalk with one swing of his hatchet. The Giant fell to the ground and died instantly!

Jack gave the golden goose to his mother, who instantly recognized it as her own beloved pet. Then he said to the harp, "Play dinner, please." A grand meal appeared before them. The very next day Jack asked the harp to play a gown for his mother, a castle to live in, and happiness to last a lifetime.

the GINGERBREAD BOY

A little old woman and a little old man once lived together in a little old house. One day the old woman made a little gingerbread boy. When she went to take him from the oven, up he jumped and away he ran!

The old woman and the old man ran after him, calling, "Stop, little Gingerbread Boy!"

But the Gingerbread Boy just laughed and sang, "Run, run as fast as you can! You can't catch me, I'm the Gingerbread Man!"

The Gingerbread Boy ran on and on until he met a cow.

"Stop!" said the Cow. "I want to eat you!"

But the little Gingerbread Boy hollered, "Run, run as fast as you can! You can't catch me, I'm the Gingerbread Man!"

Run, run as fast as you can! You can't

The Gingerbread Boy ran on until he met a horse.

"Stop!" said the Horse. "I want to eat you!"

But the little Gingerbread Boy called, "Run, run as fast as you can! You can't catch me, I'm the Gingerbread Man!"

The little Gingerbread Boy ran on until he met a pig.

"Stop!" said the Pig. "I want to eat you!"

But the little Gingerbread Boy shouted, "Run, run as fast as you can! You can't catch me, I'm the Gingerbread Man!"

The little Gingerbread Boy ran on until he met a fox.
"Hello," said the Fox politely.

Well, the little Gingerbread Boy was feeling very
bold by now, so he said to the Fox, "I've run away from
a little old woman and a little old man and a cow and a
horse and a pig, and I can run away from you, I can, I
can," and then he started to run, singing his little song,
until suddenly he stopped, for he had come to a river.

The Fox caught up to the Gingerbread Boy. "Jump on my tail and I will take you across the water," the Fox said kindly. And the Gingerbread Boy did.

After a minute the Fox said, "The water is deep. Jump on my back." And the Gingerbread Boy did.

Then in the middle of the river the Fox said, "It's getting deeper. Jump on my shoulder!" And the Gingerbread Boy did. Now when they were near the other side, the Fox cried, "The water is even deeper here! Jump on my nose!"

Now, the Gingerbread Boy knew that the minute he jumped onto the clever Fox's nose, the Fox would gobble him up. So he waited until they were almost at the shore. Then he jumped onto the Fox's nose. But before the Fox could eat him, the Gingerbread Boy jumped onto a rock, then onto dry land, and he ran away singing,

"Run, run as fast as you can!
You can't catch me,
I'm the Gingerbread Man!"

-9-

the LITTLE RED HEN

ONCE the Little Red Hen was getting

ready to plant some wheat, and she said,

"Cluck-cluck-cluck!

I'll plant this wheat all in a row,

And soon, dear friends, it will start to grow.

Now who will help me sow the wheat?"

"Not I," said the fine, feathered Duck.
"Not I," said the little gray Mouse.
"Not I," said the big pink Pig.

"Then I'll sow it all by myself," said Little Red Hen.
When the wheat had grown, Little Red Hen said,
"Now who will help me cut and thresh the wheat?"

"Not I," said the fine, feathered Duck.
"Not I," said the little gray Mouse.
"Not I," said the big pink Pig.

"Then I'll cut it and thresh it all by myself,"
said Little Red Hen.

When the wheat was cut and threshed, Little Red Hen
said, "Who'll help me carry the grain to the mill?"

"Not I," said the fine, feathered Duck.
"Not I," said the little gray Mouse.
"Not I," said the big pink Pig.

"Then I'll carry it all by myself,"
said Little Red Hen. And so she did.

When the wheat was ground,
Little Red Hen said, "Who will
help me bake the bread?"

"Not I," said the fine, feathered Duck.
"Not I," said the little gray Mouse.
"Not I," said the big pink Pig.

"Then I'll bake it all by myself,"
said Little Red Hen.

When the bread was baked, Little Red Hen said,

"The bread is done, it's warm and sweet,
Now who will come and help me eat?"

"I will!" said the fine, feathered Duck.
"I will!" said the little gray Mouse.
"I will!" said the big pink Pig.

"Oh no, you won't!" cried Little Red Hen.

"I asked for help time and again,
but no one proved to be my friend.
So I'll eat it all by myself!
Cluck-cluck!"

And so she did.

the UGLY DUCKLING

ONCE UPON A TIME, five eggs began to hatch. One by one, pretty yellow ducklings came out of their shells. But one egg was not like the others. When it cracked, out came a clumsy little gray bird with a great long neck.

The other animals in the barnyard made fun of the
Ugly Duckling. He wished he could belong, but even his
own brothers and sisters thought he was an odd duck.

So one day, when everyone was pestering him, the Ugly Duckling decided to run away.

He flew over the hedge and made a little nest for himself, all alone, at the edge of a pond.

Slowly the months passed, and the days grew colder. One evening a flock of strange birds appeared on the pond. They were dazzlingly white, with long, graceful necks.

Never had the Ugly Duckling seen such beauty.

With a strange, sharp cry, the birds spread their wings and flew off. The Ugly Duckling swam madly around on the little pond and then he, too, cried out—a strange, sharp cry. He longed to fly away with the beautiful birds.

All winter long the Ugly Duckling dreamed of those birds. Finally spring came. The little animals and flowers started stirring. One fine day the Ugly Duckling saw two beautiful white birds like those he'd dreamed of all winter.

"Look! The swans have come!" cried some children.

Our duckling was very sad. He felt even uglier and more alone than usual. But as he ducked his head, he saw himself in the water for the very first time that spring. He had a long graceful neck and dazzling white feathers. He was no longer an ugly duckling! He was a swan!

The Ugly Duckling had changed into his grown-up self! He was the same, but different, all at once. "I had no idea I would turn out this way!" said the happy new swan.

Other swans swam over to meet him. They welcomed him to their flock. The children threw bread crumbs to him and cried, "There's a beautiful new swan this year!" He had found where he belonged at last.

11

CINDERELLA

ONCE THERE WAS a girl named Ella who was good and kind and beautiful— but her stepmother was vain and selfish, and her two stepsisters were just as bad. They made Ella do all the hard work. Since she was often covered in dirt and cinders, they called her Cinderella.

One night the Prince was having a grand ball, but Cinderella's stepmother would not let her go. Alone and lonely, Cinderella began to cry. Her tears were falling freely when her fairy godmother appeared. Tapping things with her magic wand, the fairy godmother changed a pumpkin into a splendid coach. Six mice turned into horses, and a rat became the coachman.

Then the fairy godmother touched Cinderella with her wand. Instantly, instead of rags Cinderella wore a pink gown and silver slippers. Smiling, the fairy godmother said, "Do not stay late at the ball, my dear, for at the stroke of midnight, the magic will end, and all will be as it was before."

When Cinderella arrived at the ball, everyone stopped to stare. Her stepsisters, who did not recognize her, were jealous. The Prince thought Cinderella was the most beautiful woman he had ever seen, and he asked her to dance all through the night. She was having so much fun that she forgot to think about the time.

Bong! Bong! Bong! The clock began to strike midnight. Suddenly, Cinderella ran out the door and down the steps. One of her silver slippers fell off, but she kept running. As the clock struck twelve, her beautiful gown turned to rags, and her coach disappeared! All she had left was one silver slipper.

The Prince was very sad. When he found a silver slipper on the palace steps, he and his men traveled throughout the kingdom, trying the slipper on every lady's foot.

At last the slipper was brought to Cinderella's ugly stepsisters. They pinched their heels and curled their toes, but the slipper didn't fit. Then Cinderella said softly, "May I try?"

The Prince ran in to find that the slipper fit her perfectly.

When he took one look into Cinderella's good, kind face,
he knew she was his Princess. It was a grand wedding.
Cinderella and her Prince danced well past midnight,
and they enjoyed each
other's company
ever after.

−12−
ALADDIN

ONCE THERE WAS a poor young man named Aladdin who was hopelessly in love with a Sultan's daughter. Whenever Princess Aria passed by, his heart stopped. Aladdin knew that a poor boy could never win a Sultan's daughter, but he swore that he would never love another.

Next to the
Princess, what
Aladdin loved most
was exploring. One day
he discovered a hidden cave,
and inside he found an old oil lamp.
This was no ordinary lamp—it had been
hidden in the cave by a wicked and
powerful magician.

It was a dusty thing, and Aladdin
began to polish it with his sleeve. All
of a sudden . . . WHOOSH! A burst of
light filled the cave, and out of the
lamp a genie appeared.

"Master of the lamp," the genie
boomed. "What is your wish?"

Aladdin was astonished!
And he knew just what to
ask for. He said, "I wish
for a gift fine enough
for Princess Aria."

No sooner had he said the words than Aladdin found himself surrounded by riches. "Your wish is my command," said the genie. "What else do you desire?"

Aladdin wished for fine clothes and a good steed.

Soon dressed in princely clothes and riding a fine stallion, he was off to the Sultan's palace.

The Sultan and his daughter were charmed by Aladdin's friendly smile. After an enchanting afternoon, Princess Aria agreed to marry him.

Aladdin commanded the genie to build them a grand palace, and in an instant it was done. Happy beyond measure, Aladdin still told no one, not even his dear Aria, about the magic lamp.

One day, when Aladdin was away, the Princess found the dusty lamp high on a shelf. Hours later a peddler came walking through the streets crying, "New lamps for old! New lamps for old!"

"Will you take even this old tarnished one?" the Princess asked.

"Certainly!" came the reply. For this man was not a peddler; he was the wicked magician who had hidden the lamp in the cave. And he was determined to get it back.

As soon as he held the lamp, he rubbed it, and the genie appeared. "Carry this palace and all of us in it far into the desert," the magician commanded. In an instant, only bare ground remained where the palace had stood.

When Aladdin returned home, he realized at once what must have happened. Without wasting a minute, he set out to find and rescue Princess Aria.

After wandering the desert for weeks, Aladdin discovered the palace. He snuck inside and surprised his bride. Aria was overcome with joy to see him.

"We must get the lamp," said Aladdin. The Princess said, "It's always by his side."

So that night, as the magician slept, Aladdin crept into his room. He took the lamp and made a wish. When the magician awoke, he was asleep in the sand!

Back in the city, Aladdin and the Princess thanked
the genie for all his help. The Sultan was so happy
that he gave Aladdin half his kingdom. From then
on, Aladdin used the lamp only to do good for his
people, and he shared his great riches with the poor.

SNOW WHITE and the SEVEN DWARFS

ONCE THERE WAS a lovely princess called Snow White. Her stepmother, the queen, was beautiful but very vain. The Queen loved to look into her magic mirror and say:

Mirror, mirror on the wall,

Who is fairest of us all?

And the mirror always said:
Queen, you are fairest of us all.
But Snow White grew more beautiful as she grew older, and one day the mirror said:

Queen, thou art fairest that I see,
But Snow White is more fair than thee.

Furious, the Queen called to her guard and ordered him to kill Snow White.

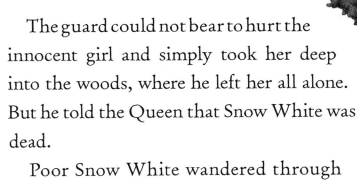

The guard could not bear to hurt the innocent girl and simply took her deep into the woods, where he left her all alone. But he told the Queen that Snow White was dead.

Poor Snow White wandered through the frightening woods for a long while.

At last she came to a little cottage.

She knocked timidly at the door—and was surprised when it was opened by the tiniest person she had ever seen!

The cottage was owned by seven friendly dwarfs. When they learned what the wicked Queen had done to Snow White, they offered to let her live with them.

Snow White agreed, and they settled into a happy routine. Each morning the dwarfs would go off to work, and each evening they would return to warm supper and a house as neat as a pin.

All the while, the Queen believed Snow White was dead. Then one day she stood in front of her magic mirror and said those familiar words:

Mirror, mirror on the wall,
Who is fairest of us all?
And the mirror answered:
Queen, thou art fairest that I see,
But Snow White living in the glen
With the seven little men
Is a thousand times more fair than thee.

Imagine how shocked and angry the Queen was!
With magic spells she created a poisonous apple.

Then she disguised herself as an old peddler and
set off for the seven dwarfs' cottage. Once there, she
called out, "Apples for sale. Delicious apples."

Snow White told the old woman she had no money.

"For one so pretty as you, the apple is free," the old
woman said.

Snow White could not resist. She took the apple and bit into it. As soon as she did, she fell down, still and cold.

The Queen laughed with glee and disappeared into the woods.

When the seven dwarfs came home, they were heartbroken to find their dear Snow White lying there.

She looked too beautiful to bury, so they placed
her in a glass coffin atop a high hill. Each dwarf took
a turn keeping watch.

Snow White lay there for a long, long time. But
her appearance never changed. She seemed only to be
sleeping.

One day, a king's son rode by and was charmed by
Snow White's beauty. He begged the dwarfs to move the
coffin so he could see her better. As they picked it up, the
bit of apple fell out of her mouth and she awoke.

Seeing Snow White's lovely face made the Prince joyful.
They walked and talked and soon fell in love.

The seven dwarfs were the guests of honor at the grand celebration of their marriage. A great feast was held, and Snow White danced with everyone. Before the night ended, she and the Prince made the dwarfs promise to visit them often at the castle.

And so they all lived happily ever after.

—14—
the FROG PRINCE

ONCE YOU COULD always find the Princess alone, playing with her golden ball by the pond on the castle grounds. One day she missed her catch, and the ball landed in the pond and sank.

The Princess didn't want to wade in to get the ball. She didn't want to get wet! So she began to cry.

A small green frog asked, "What will you give me if I get the ball for you?"

"You can have anything you want," she said.

"What I want is simply to be your friend. I want to sit with you at supper and eat from your plate. I want to listen as you read aloud from a book and to sleep on your pillow after you kiss me good night."

Well, the Princess was sure her father the King would not welcome a warty old frog to dinner, but she promised anyway. As soon as the Frog brought her the golden ball, the Princess skipped away to the palace, ignoring the Frog's ribbet-y cries to wait for him.

By dinnertime, the Frog had hopped all the way to the castle, where he called out for the Princess.

"What would a frog want with you?" the King asked his daughter.

And so the Princess told him she'd promised the Frog she'd be his friend if only he would return the golden ball to her.

"A promise made must be kept," said the King.

So the Frog joined the royal family for dinner.
He ate from the young princess's plate and
drank from her cup. After dinner, the Princess
read to him from her storybook.
Much to the Princess's surprise,
the Frog was good company,
and they passed a
pleasant evening
together.

At bedtime the Princess carried the Frog up the
stairs and set him on her pillow. But she had no wish
to share her pillow with a frog, even a nice frog. So
she said, "You may sleep on my pillow. I will gladly
sleep here on the floor." She kissed him on his knobby
head and said, "Good night, my dear Froggy."

In that instant, the Frog turned into a handsome Prince. The Princess could not believe her eyes, but the Prince explained that a witch had put a spell on him, and the Princess was the first to break it with a kiss.

Now they could play and talk for hours, and they grew to be very fond of each other. Best of all, the Princess had someone to play catch with—and they never tired of tossing each other the golden ball that had brought them together.

-15-
the LITTLE MERMAID

OUT AT SEA, there lived a good mer-king with his six daughters in a palace made of coral and shells. Happy in their underwater kingdom, the mermaid princesses played among the flowers on the sea floor. Only the youngest wondered what it would be like to walk on land.

One day, after a shipwreck, the Little Mermaid rescued the only survivor, a handsome prince. The Little Mermaid pulled the Prince to the shore—but there she had to leave him. She could not go on land herself. Instead she kept watch from the waves a short distance away.

The next morning, a lovely girl came across the Prince asleep on the beach. When he awoke, he thought that this girl had saved him. He remembered nothing of the Little Mermaid.

But the Little Mermaid could not forget the Prince.

She returned to the edge of the shore every day, hoping to see him. She wanted to be with him, but she knew that a prince would never love a princess with a fish's tail.

So the Little Mermaid went to visit the Old Witch of the Sea.

"My help comes with a high price," said the Witch, giving the Little Mermaid a small bottle. "If you drink this potion, you will become human, but you will lose your voice. And if the Prince does not marry you, you will turn to sea foam and disappear forever." Unafraid, the Little Mermaid drank the potion and fainted dead away.

When she awoke in human form, she saw the Prince but could not speak. Seeing that she needed help, the Prince took her to his castle. From that day on, the Little Mermaid was happy just to be near him.

But the Prince decided to marry the girl he believed had rescued him from the sea.

The Little Mermaid could not
speak to tell him the truth. When she saw how
happy he was, she did not want to.

On the night of the wedding, the Little
Mermaid walked along the shore, staring out
to sea. Through her tears, she saw her sisters rise
up through the waves. "We have come from the
Old Witch of the Sea," one said. "If you kill the
Prince before sunrise, you may return to the
world under the waves."

Then they handed her a magic dagger.

Of course, the Little Mermaid could not harm the Prince. She threw away the dagger and jumped into the sea. She expected to turn into foam, but instead, she felt herself rising into the air, surrounded by friendly spirits. "You have done many kind things for others," the spirits said. "Come stay with us, and be happy forever."

At once, the Little Mermaid was happy. She had dreamed of walking, but now she could fly.

-16-
the PRINCESS
and the PEA

ONCE UPON A TIME, there was a prince who wanted more than anything to fall in love and get married. But though he met one princess after another, there was always something not quite right.

"They just aren't real princesses," he said. "They aren't real princesses at all!"

"What is a real princess?" asked his father, the King.

"Her hair will shine, her nose will be regal, but the princess part will be in her eyes. They'll sparkle," said the Prince.

"And fine! A princess will be fine," added his mother, who had once been a princess herself, of course.

Now, one evening a wild storm broke over the kingdom. Suddenly there came a knock at the palace door. Outside stood a girl, soaking wet from head to toe.

"Who are you?" asked the King.

"I am Princess Adriana and I got separated from my companions in the storm," she said.

The Prince came running. It was hard to see if she was a real princess. Her nose looked regal, but water dripped from the tip of it. And her eyes—the Prince could hardly see them behind the mop of wet hair.

Now the Queen knew that a true princess would be very, very delicate, and she thought of a way to test the girl's claim. She gathered all the mattresses and quilts from all the beds in the palace and stacked them up.

Then she secretly tucked a tiny pea under the bottom mattress and bid the girl good night.

When the girl came downstairs in the morning, she was a lovely sight to see. Her hair flowed long and wavy, washed clean from the rain. Her nose was just as regal as could be. And when she looked up—

"Your eyes! They're so sparkly!" said the Prince.

"But you are yawning!" said the Queen. "Didn't you sleep well, my dear?"

"You were wonderful to take me in, and I don't like to complain," said the girl, "but I did not sleep a wink! There was a lump in the bed, and I'm afraid it kept me awake all night."

"Aha!" cried the Queen. "You are a real princess! Only a real princess could be fine enough to feel a pea through twenty mattresses!"

The Prince quickly fell in love with the Princess. In time they got married and the Prince started making the bed every day, careful to smooth out any lumps or wrinkles so that his dear Princess would enjoy a good night's sleep.

~17~
RAPUNZEL

NE DAY, a witch stole a little baby from her parents. She named the girl Rapunzel and locked her in a tall tower deep in the woods. The tower had no door, no stairs, and only a small window at the top. Rapunzel lived alone there for many years. Her golden hair grew so long it reached the ground.

When the Witch wanted to visit, she would stand below the window and shout, "Rapunzel, Rapunzel! Let down your hair!"

Rapunzel would lower her long golden braid, and the Witch would use it as a rope to climb the tower wall.

One day, a king's son rode nearby when Rapunzel was singing to her only companions, the birds. Hearing Rapunzel's beautiful voice, he drew closer to the tower. He was just in time to see the Witch arrive and hear her shout, "Rapunzel, Rapunzel! Let down your hair!"

Hiding behind a tree, the Prince saw the golden braid cascade down from the window for the Witch to climb.

As soon as the Witch had gone, the Prince hurried to the foot of
the tower and called, "Rapunzel, Rapunzel! Let down your hair!"

Rapunzel was surprised and delighted to see a young prince.
She welcomed him happily.

The Prince returned every evening to visit, and as they talked
and sang together, they fell in love. They planned to marry as
soon as Rapunzel could escape from the tower.

But one day, when Rapunzel was lost in dreams, she forgot herself and foolishly asked the Witch, "Why do you climb so much slower than my Prince?"

Realizing she'd been tricked, the Witch grew furious.

She took out a big pair of scissors
and lopped off Rapunzel's long
braid with one mighty snip.
Then she took Rapunzel to
a faraway wilderness and left
her there, all alone.

That evening, the Witch returned to the tower.
When the Prince called, "Rapunzel, Rapunzel! Let
down your hair!" the braid came tumbling down
as usual. But when the Prince reached the window,
there was the Witch!

"Your sweet songbird has left the nest," she
screeched. "You'll never see her again!" She pushed
the Prince out of the tower, and he fell into a patch of
briars that scratched out his eyes.

Blind and lonely, the Prince wandered far and wide, always searching for Rapunzel. He'd nearly given up hope when one day he heard a soft, sad song that he recognized from long ago.

Running toward the sound, he cried out, "Rapunzel!" Rapunzel fell against him, crying tears of happiness. And what happened then was truly magical. When her tears fell into his eyes, he found he could see again! What he saw was his one true love.

Soon Rapunzel and her Prince
were married. Her hair once
again grew long, and her
joyous song filled their
castle like sunshine.

18

THUMBELINA

ONCE UPON A TIME, a tiny maiden named Thumbelina lived in a garden. She made her home under a flower. Her bed was a walnut shell, and she had a rose leaf for a blanket. Thumbelina loved living in the garden. All of the bumblebees and dragonflies were her friends.

One night, a toad crept through the garden, saw Thumbelina sleeping, and thought, What a pretty little wife she will make for my son! Picking up the bed with Thumbelina in it, the toad hopped away.

When Thumbelina awoke, she found herself on a lily pad far out in a stream. Two large toads were staring at her. The older one told Thumbelina, "Meet my son. He will be your husband."

"Croak, croak!" her son said, tipping his hat.

Thumbelina couldn't bear to think of marrying the toad. As the mother and son swam away, she began to cry. Luckily fish had been listening nearby, and they felt sorry for Thumbelina. They sent her lily pad floating downstream.

Thumbelina sailed past many towns, finally reaching a beautiful country.

There she wove a bed from blades of grass, drank the dew from the leaves, and ate the honey from the flowers. When the first snow came, Thumbelina took shelter with a field mouse.

One day, the mouse took Thumbelina to call on a very rich neighbor, the mole. As they walked through a tunnel to his grand underground home, they came across a dead swallow. Thumbelina was very sad, but the mole just said, "How glad I am not to be a bird." He ordered his workers to cover up the hole in the tunnel roof through which the swallow had fallen.

That night Thumbelina could not sleep. Taking a blanket, she crept out of bed to the tunnel. "Farewell, dear one," she whispered. Spreading the warm blanket over the swallow's cold body, she laid her head on the bird's breast. But what do you think she heard then? The thump of a heartbeat! The bird was not really dead, only frozen, and the blanket had warmed him back to life.

All that winter and on into spring, Thumbelina secretly visited the swallow, bringing him food and drink. Then one day she rushed to him crying, "The mole wants to marry me!"

Knowing that Thumbelina didn't want to marry the mole any more than she had wanted to marry the toad, the swallow said, "Fly away with me."

Thumbelina quickly agreed. She climbed on his back, and away they flew!

After many days, the bird set Thumbelina down gently in a field of flowers. As tiny people who lived among the blossoms rushed up and welcomed her, Thumbelina felt warm and happy. Finally she had come home.

19

RUMPELSTILTSKIN

ONCE A MILLER bragged about his lovely daughter to the King. He claimed that she could do anything! "She can even spin straw into gold!" The miller didn't mean to lie; it just popped out.

"Bring her to my castle," said the King hastily. "My advisers demand more gold."

So the Miller brought his daughter to the castle. When the King saw her, he fell in love, but his advisers locked the poor girl in a room full of straw, saying, "Spin this straw into gold by morning. If you cannot, then your father will be put to death for lying to the King."

The poor girl knew she couldn't spin that straw into gold. When she began to cry, a tiny little man appeared. He promised to spin the gold if she would give him something in return.

"My necklace?" the girl offered.

The little man agreed, and in no time he spun all the straw into gold.

The King was amazed and thanked the girl, but his advisers locked her into an even bigger room full of straw and demanded more gold.

Once more the tiny little man appeared. Again he promised to spin the gold in return for something.

"My ring?" the girl offered.

The little man agreed, and again he spun every bit of straw into gold.

The King was thrilled, but his advisers demanded more gold. 'Fine,' he said, "but if she spins the gold again, I'll make her my Queen."

Again the little man appeared, but now the girl had nothing left to give him.

"I will spin the gold," said the little man, "if you promise to give me your firstborn child." The girl believed she would never have a child because she thought the advisers would never let her marry.

"Very well," she said. "I agree."

When the King's advisers saw all the gold, they were delighted.
And when the King embraced the Miller's daughter, he swore that
he would love her always. They were married, and in time the new
Queen gave birth to a baby boy, who was the joy of her life. But on
the boy's first birthday, the tiny little man appeared once more.

The Queen begged and pleaded to keep
her child. The little man finally agreed to
release her from her promise only if she
could guess his name in three days' time.
On the first day, the Queen tried
name after name, but to each the little
man shook his head. On the second
day, the Queen sent her servants out
to gather every name in the kingdom.
Still, she couldn't guess.

On the third day, she had almost given up hope when one of her handmaids came running into the room. She had been walking in the woods when she overheard the little man singing:

What a most delightful game,
Oh, Rumpelstiltskin is my name!

That evening, the little man came to claim his prize. The Queen asked, "Is your name Peter?"

"No," he replied.

"John?"

"No."

"Ralph?"

"No!"

"Albert?"

"No!!"

Now the Queen smiled. "Is it . . . Rumpelstiltskin?"

At that, Rumpelstiltskin stamped his little feet and flew into a rage.

He ran away as fast as his legs could carry him, and he was never seen again.

–20–
SLEEPING BEAUTY

N THE OCCASION of their first baby's birth, a king and queen invited six good fairies to a party. They forgot to invite the seventh fairy!

At the party, the fairies began to give gifts to the Princess. The first wished her wisdom. The second, a kind heart. The third, great beauty.

And so it went up through the fifth fairy, with each one offering a gift to assure the Princess a happy life.

Suddenly the door to the castle flew open. It was the seventh fairy, and she was furious.

"Now I will give my gift to the Princess," she said. "When she is fifteen years old, she will prick her finger on a spinning wheel and fall down dead."

Then the angry fairy stormed out of the room.

The King and Queen were terribly upset. But then the sixth fairy, who was the youngest of all, stepped forward.

"I have not yet given my gift," she said. "I cannot change the wicked curse, but I can soften it. The Princess will not die but instead will fall into a deep sleep. She will awaken only when her true love kisses her."

The King was grateful to the young fairy but still worried. Trying to avoid the curse, he decreed that every spinning wheel in the kingdom be burned in a great fire.

Many years passed, and just as the good fairies wished, the Princess grew to be kind and smart and beautiful. The wicked curse was all but forgotten.

On the day she turned fifteen, the Princess decided to explore the castle. Coming to a tower she'd never seen before, she climbed its winding staircase and opened the door at the top. Inside was a woman sitting at a spinning wheel. The Princess didn't know it, but the woman was the wicked fairy in disguise.

"What are you doing?" asked the Princess. She had never seen a spinning wheel, since they had all been burned.

"I'm spinning flax into thread," said the woman, smiling. "Would you like to try?"

The Princess sat down at the spinning wheel, but no sooner had she touched it than she pricked her finger on the sharp spindle. Instantly, she fell into a deep sleep.

In fact, the angry fairy's spell was so strong that dogs stopped barking, flies stopped buzzing, and curtains stopped flapping in the breeze. The King and Queen and every creature in the castle fell asleep. A tangled hedge of thorns grew around the castle walls, so thick that no one could enter.

And then one day, a hundred years later,
a prince came riding by. Although many
men had tried and failed to fight
their way through the hedge,
this prince was special. He
was Beauty's true love.
As he approached the
hedge, its branches
parted and he rode
straight to the
castle.

Everywhere he looked, he saw people and animals
fast asleep.

He tiptoed among them until, finally, he found the
sleeping Princess in the tower.

He thought she was so beautiful that he leaned over and kissed her cheek. And just like that, the spell was broken.

Opening her eyes, the Princess said, "I dreamed you would come." Then she took his hand, and they came down from the tower to find the whole kingdom waking up.

The King and the Queen were so overjoyed that they planned a great feast to at last celebrate the Princess's sixteenth birthday. And this time, they made sure to invite every single fairy in the wood.

For my mother and father.

Mary Engelbreit's Nursery and Fairy Tales Storybook Favorites,
originally published as *Mary Engelbreit's Nursery and Fairy Tales Collection*
Copyright © 2008, 2010, and 2014 by Mary Engelbreit Ink

ISBN 978-0-06-294266-1

Design by Stephanie Bart-Horvath
20 21 22 23 24 SCP 10 9 8 7 6 5 4 3 2 1
❖

HARPER
An Imprint of HarperCollins*Publishers*   www.harpercollinschildrens.com   Illustrations © Mary Engelbreit Ink